Dear Parents:

Congratulations! Your child is taking the first steps on an exciting journey. The destination? Independent reading!

STEP INTO READING® will help your child get there. The program offers five steps to reading success. Each step includes fun stories and colorful art or photographs. In addition to original fiction and books with favorite characters, there are Step into Reading Non-Fiction Readers, Phonics Readers and Boxed Sets, Sticker Readers, and Comic Readers—a complete literacy program with something to interest every child.

Learning to Read, Step by Step!

Ready to Read   Preschool–Kindergarten
• big type and easy words • rhyme and rhythm • picture clues
For children who know the alphabet and are eager to begin reading.

Reading with Help   Preschool–Grade 1
• basic vocabulary • short sentences • simple stories
For children who recognize familiar words and sound out new words with help.

Reading on Your Own   Grades 1–3
• engaging characters • easy-to-follow plots • popular topics
For children who are ready to read on their own.

Reading Paragraphs   Grades 2–3
• challenging vocabulary • short paragraphs • exciting stories
For newly independent readers who read simple sentences with confidence.

Ready for Chapters   Grades 2–4
• chapters • longer paragraphs • full-color art
For children who want to take the plunge into chapter books but still like colorful pictures.

STEP INTO READING® is designed to give every child a successful reading experience. The grade levels are only guides; children will progress through the steps at their own speed, developing confidence in their reading. The F&P Text Level on the back cover serves as another tool to help you choose the right book for your child.

Remember, a lifetime love of reading starts with a single step!

For Christopher and Annie

Step into Reading, Random House, and the Random House colophon are registered trademarks of Penguin Random House LLC.

Visit us on the Web!
StepIntoReading.com
randomhousekids.com

Educators and librarians, for a variety of teaching tools, visit us at
RHTeachersLibrarians.com

Library of Congress Cataloging-in-Publication Data
Weston, Martha.
Jack and Jill and Big Dog Bill : a phonics reader / by Martha Weston. p. cm. —
(Step into reading. A step 1 book)
Summary: Jack and Jill enjoy sledding until their dog gets tired.
ISBN 978-0-375-81248-4 (trade) — ISBN 978-0-375-91248-1 (lib. bdg.)
[1. Dogs—Fiction. 2. Sleds—Fiction.]
I. Title. II. Step into reading. Step 1 book.
PZ7.W52645 Jae 2003 [E]—dc21 2002013223

Printed in the United States of America 38 37 36 35 34 33 32 31 30

This book has been officially leveled by using the F&P Text Level Gradient™ Leveling System.

Jack and Jill and Big Dog Bill

by Martha Weston

Random House 🏠 New York

Jack and Jill
and Big Dog Bill
go up, up, up the hill.

"Pull, Bill!" says Jill.

At the top,
they stop.

"Go, Bill!" say
Jack and Jill.
So Jack and Jill
and Big Dog Bill
go down, down, down
the hill.

BUMP.

PLOP.

They all stop.

"More, more!" says Jack.

Jack and Jill
and Big Dog Bill
go up, up, up the hill.

"Push, Bill!" says Jill.

At the top,
they stop.

"Go, Bill!" says Jill.

Jack and Jill
and Big Dog Bill
go down, down, down
the hill.

BUMP.

PLOP.

They all stop.

"More!" says Jack.

"More!" says Jill.

"Oh, no," say Jack
and Jill.
"Bill will not go!"

Jack and Jill
and Big Dog Bill
go up, up, up the hill.

"Push, Jack!" says Jill.

"Pull, Jill!" says Jack.

At the top,
they stop.

Jack and Jill
and Big Dog Bill
go down, down, down
the hill.

BUMP.

PLOP.

They all stop.

"No more hill!"

say Jack and Jill.

Jack and Jill
and Big Dog Bill
go home.